WITHDRAWN
BY
WILLIAMSBURG REGIONAL LIBRARY

Pete the Cat's

Groovy Guide to

LOVE

Tips from **A COOL CAT** on how to spread the **LOVE**

by Kimberly & James Dean

HARPER

An Imprint of HarperCollinsPublishers

Williamsburg Regional Library
757-259-4040   www.wrl.org

FEB - - 2016

Pete the Cat's Groovy Guide to Love
Text copyright © 2015 by Kimberly and James Dean
Illustrations copyright © 2015 by James Dean
All rights reserved. Printed in the United States of America. No part of this book may be used
or reproduced in any manner whatsoever without written permission except in the case of
brief quotations embodied in critical articles and reviews. For information address
HarperCollins Children's Books, a division of HarperCollins Publishers, 195 Broadway, New York, NY 10007.
www.harpercollinschildrens.com
ISBN 978-0-06-243061-8
The artist used pen and ink, with watercolor and acrylic paint,
on 300lb hot press paper to create the illustrations for this book.
Typography by Jeanne L. Hogle
15 16 17 18 19 PC 10 9 8 7 6 5 4 3 2 1
❖
First Edition

For my family, who bring me so much joy
and unconditional love!
1 Corinthians 13:13
—K.D.

For Kim.
I love cats and I love art.
I love you with all my heart.
—J.D.

"Love is a friendship set to music."

—JOSEPH CAMPBELL

"A loving heart was better and stronger than wisdom." —CHARLES DICKENS

"Love yourself and everything else falls into line." —LUCILLE BALL

"Love is the greatest refreshment in life."

—PABLO PICASSO

**"At the touch of love,
everyone becomes a poet."**

—PLATO

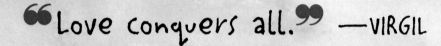 "Love conquers all." —VIRGIL

"Where love is concerned, too much is not even enough." —PIERRE BEAUMARCHAIS

"Love is the master key which opens the gates of happiness.99

—OLIVER WENDELL HOLMES

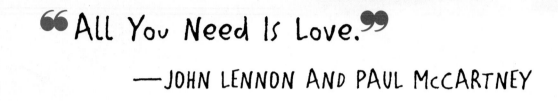

"All You Need Is Love."

—JOHN LENNON AND PAUL McCARTNEY

"The best thing to hold on to in life is each other."

—AUDREY HEPBURN

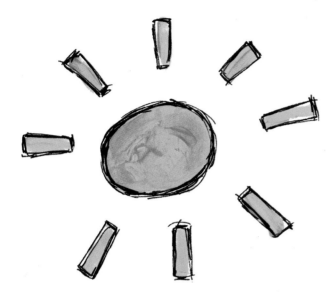

"Let the beauty of what you love be what you do."

—RUMI

"Spread love everywhere you go. Let no one ever come to you without leaving happier.**"** —MOTHER TERESA

"Keep love in your heart. A life without it is like a sunless garden when the flowers are dead."

—OSCAR WILDE

"Where there is love there is life."

—MAHATMA GANDHI

"Love is patient, love is kind. It does not envy, it does not boast, it is not proud."

—1 CORINTHIANS 13:4–8

"Being deeply loved by someone gives you strength, while loving someone deeply gives you courage."

—LAO TZU

Love makes
you brave.
—PETE

"How do I love thee?
Let me count the ways."

—ELIZABETH BARRETT BROWNING

❝The way to know life is to love many things.**❞**

—VINCENT VAN GOGH

"If you want to be loved, be lovable."

—OVID

"The first duty of love is to listen." —PAUL TILLICH

A cool friend is a good listener.
—PETE

"May the sun shine all day long, everything go right and nothing wrong. May those you love bring love back to you, and may all the wishes you wish come true!"

—IRISH BLESSING